D1589091

THE ADVENTURES OF

THE SAD CLOWN

Story by Rosie Alison

Pictures by Atholl McDonald

For Lucy & Daisy: R.A.
For Cairn & Brodie: A.M.

This edition published in 2003 by
The Rose Press, Daisy and Tom, Granville House,
2a Pond Place, London SW3 6QJ

Reprinted 2005

Copyright © Text Rosie Alison

Illustrations by Atholl McDonald

The moral right of the author has been asserted

A CIP catalogue record of this book is available from
the British Library

ISBN: 1 - 901503 - 02 -X

Manufactured in China by Imago

Daisy and Tom are twins with a wonderful secret: they have a magic kite called Oscar, who carries them off on adventures to mysterious new lands.

Time and again they fly off together, knowing that Oscar will always bring them safely back home in the end.

One Saturday morning, Daisy and Tom awoke to see great clouds rolling slowly past their house. After a busy week at school, they could hardly wait to explore them with Oscar.

As soon as breakfast was over, they raced out into the fields with their magic kite. In a moment, they were sailing through the sky with Oscar, flying far above the sheep and trees, until they broke right through the clouds into a whole new world ...

"Wherever can we be?" asked Daisy. Oscar had brought them to a strange land of lollipop trees and candystick canes. Far away, they could see the striped tents of a fairground. "Come on!" said Tom, "let's follow this road and see what happens."

"Do you see what I see?" whispered Daisy. Trotting towards them was a carousel horse, with a jaunty monkey perched on his back.

"Good morning to you! Are you lost?" asked the monkey, raising his hat politely. Tom explained that they had come in search of adventure.

"I'm Cosmo," said the monkey, "and this is Woody, the Carousel Horse. We're both from the Faraway Fair," he added, pointing over the hill.

"Where are you going?" asked Daisy.

"We're out looking for a missing clown," replied Cosmo, swinging from Woody's pole.

"It's our friend Caspar," explained Woody, "he's run away from the Fair. Today is Clown Day, when hundreds of clowns gather at the fairground for a Grand Competition. Caspar is the youngest of the famous Corelli Clowns, and he's disappeared. We must find him before the Clown Show begins."

Daisy and Tom were quick to offer their help, so they all set off together in search of Caspar. It wasn't long before they came to an old forgotten fairground, perched on the edge of a steep gulley. And there, lying on a dusty track, was a red unicycle.

"Heeelp!"

Suddenly, they heard a faint cry rising from the gulley below. Leaning over the edge, they could see a yellow-hatted clown clinging to a zig zag tree.

"Heeelp!" he cried. "I fell off my unicycle and toppled over!"

Quickly, Oscar flew to the rescue, taking his string down to Caspar.

"Hang onto our kite, and he'll soon pull you up!" called Daisy. A moment later, Caspar was lifted from danger.

The young clown sat on a rock, and thanked them all.
But there were tears in his eyes.

"Why did you run away?" asked Woody, very gently.

Caspar gave a great sigh and looked down.

"Because nobody wants a sad clown. I do so want to
make people laugh, but I just can't do it. I'm too shy to
sing or dance. I can't even ride my unicycle."

"Why don't you let Oscar help you?" suggested Daisy, wrapping the kite string around Caspar's middle.

Suddenly, with Oscar supporting him, Caspar was no longer scared of riding his unicycle. Round and round they went, until Oscar gently unwound himself and let Caspar ride alone.

"I can do it! I can do it by myself!" cried Caspar, raising his arms, and laughing.

N ow it was Cosmo's turn to help.

"Just watch me!" he called, and started to juggle. Caspar was beginning to enjoy himself, so everything became easier. He copied Cosmo, and in no time he too was juggling ...

... and turning cartwheels ...

... and walking on his hands. With a little confidence, he was no longer a sad clown - he was a clown who could make people happy!

"We must get you back in time for the Clown Show!" called Woody, rounding them all up. He led them away from the forgotten fairground until they saw the Faraway Fair blazing with colour in the valley beyond.

Mr Corelli was delighted to see his son Caspar returned. He thanked Daisy and Tom warmly, and gave them tickets for the Clown Show. Full of hope, Caspar took his father aside.

"Please can I be in the show today?" he asked. His father looked at him carefully, then gently shook his head.

"I'm so sorry Caspar, but I don't think you're ready for this yet. Maybe next year."

Caspar wanted to be brave, but he was a picture of sadness. Daisy and Tom tried to cheer him up but it was no use, not even Cosmo's cartwheels could make him smile.

But by now it was time for the Clown Show, so Woody hurried the twins towards an enormous circus tent, along with a great crowd of clowns.

CIRCUS

WOODY

"Where's Caspar got to?" wondered Tom, looking round.

Cosmo found some good seats for the twins, and they watched happily as clowns of every shape and size performed their routines. When the famous Corelli Clowns appeared, Tom asked again, "Where is Caspar?"

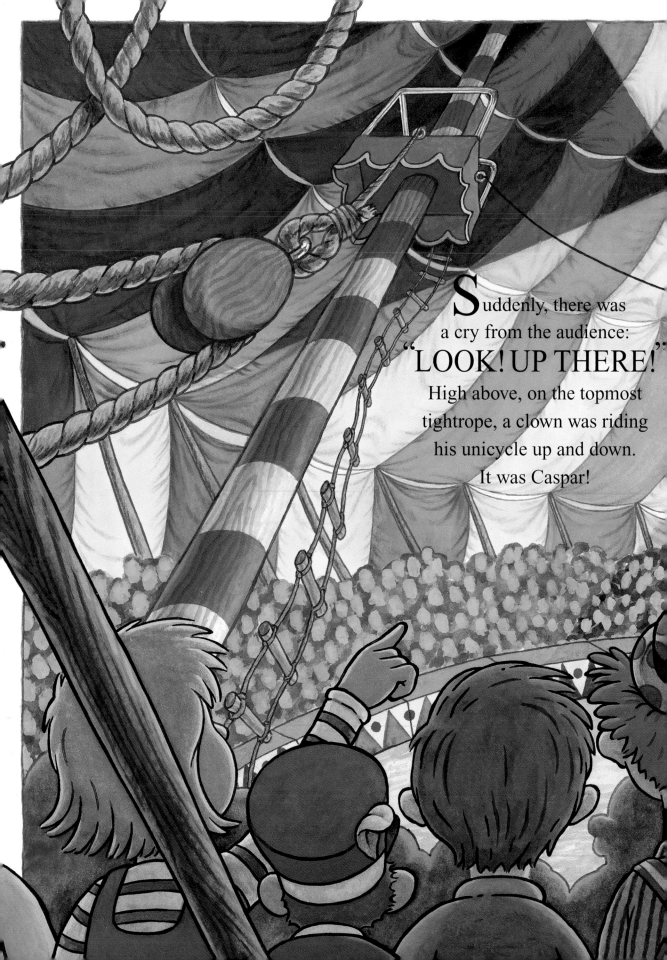

Suddenly, there was
a cry from the audience:
"LOOK! UP THERE!"
High above, on the topmost
tightrope, a clown was riding
his unicycle up and down.
It was Caspar!

The clowns all cheered as Caspar swung down, and went on to steal the show,

… dancing …

… and diving …

…and tumbling …

… and juggling …

… until everyone stood and clapped the brilliant young clown.

"We have a new star," announced the Judges, and they gave Caspar three Golden Skittles as a prize for his performance.

Caspar's father rushed forward to hug him.
"I should have guessed that you would be the King of the Corelli's!" he told him proudly. At last, Caspar was happy.

To celebrate, Caspar took Daisy and Tom all around the Fair. They met tin soldiers and a dancing pig, and even Punch and Judy out for a stroll with their crocodile. Finally, Woody gave them all a wonderful ride on the Carousel.

By now, the twins were tired and ready to go home. Even Oscar was sleepy. They said a fond goodbye to their new friends.

"Thank you," said Caspar, "for helping me not to be shy."

Then Oscar floated them gently home until they landed just by their garden gate.

They ran inside, where their parents were making a cup of tea.

"You must be hungry, after flying your kite all day!" said their mother, filling up the kettle.

"I have a surprise for you," said their father, and he held out something for them to see. Daisy and Tom grinned at each other.

"Tickets for the circus - thank you!"

P erhaps they
would bump into Caspar
again ...